TO THE LITTLE SCHOOL

FROM Carita

ON May 7, 1998

47 YEARS OLD

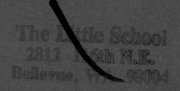

E   Paschkis, Julie
P   Play all day

                                    ✓

10054

The Little School
2812 116th N.E.
Bellevue, WA 98004

DEMCO

Play All Day

To the Little School Library

[signature]

for
Max

Julie Paschkis

Play All Day

Little, Brown and Company
Boston New York Toronto London

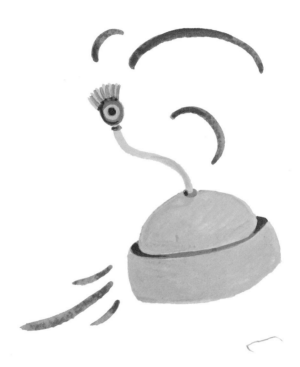

It is windy today
when I go out to play.
A blustery gust
blows my hat far away.

Giddy-up red mare!
My hat's over there.
Did a wind wizard toss it
on a branch that was bare?

My hat's back at last.
I kick my ball past
a swarm of bright bugs
in the cool, waving grass.

I see my cat spy me
ever so slyly.
I put my ball down, but
he walks right on by me.

He is off to a land
where he's a cat king so grand.
A bird serenades him
while perched on my hand.

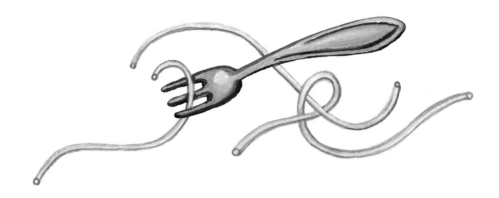

My plate is set down
by the cup with a clown.
I twirl ropes of pasta
that slither around.

I try to keep steady
as I walk on spaghetti.
Beneath the big table
my circus is ready.

I read, then I rest.
My book is the best.
It tells of a princess
who passed every test.

As a knight, I stand tall
by the great castle wall.
These old books hold secrets,
and I guard them all.

"Look, look," said Sam as he pointed at the cat with green eyes.

"Listen, listen," said Zöe as she tiptoed toward the bird with red wings.

At the end of the day,
I wash while I play.
Swirling the water
makes my boat sail away.

As the waves lift,
I feel the tides shift.
Deep under the sea,
I watch my boat drift.

Good night and sleep tight.
Out goes the light.
From my bed I can see
a star shining bright.

The moon rises high
as we float through the sky.
I pretend I'm asleep
while the bright stars glide by.

First Edition

Library of Congress Cataloging-in-Publication Data

Paschkis, Julie.
    Play all day / Julie Paschkis. — 1st ed.
        p.   cm.
    Summary: A child's day of play is both in the real world
and in the world of the imagination.
    ISBN 0-316-69043-0
    [1. Imagination — Fiction. 2. Play — Fiction. 3. Stories in
rhyme.] I. Title.
    PZ8.3.P2716Pl 1998
    [E] — DC20   96-14234

                    10 9 8 7 6 5 4 3 2 1

                              SC

            Published simultaneously in Canada
        by Little, Brown & Company (Canada) Limited

                    Printed in Hong Kong

            The paintings in this book were done in
        Winsor & Newton gouache on Arches paper.
            The display type was set in Jimbo Bold.
            The text type was set in Shannon Bold.